ELSEWHERE AND THE CLOWNS

James Roose–Evans

Collander Moll is at it again – spring cleaning.
Just when Odd and Elsewhere are beginning to
feel thoroughly upset by all the commotion
Elsewhere receives a letter from the King of the
Clowns inviting him to a Gathering of the Clowns
at Tippity House. Elsewhere wouldn't dream of
missing it as gatherings are very special, once-
in-a-lifetime occasions. But when he performs
before the King his act goes disastrously wrong.
Elsewhere nearly gives in to despair until Odd
comes to the rescue, just in the nick of time!

JAMES ROOSE-EVANS

ELSEWHERE & THE

CLOWNS

AN ODD & ELSEWHERE STORY WITH PICTURES BY BRIAN ROBB

A Magnet Book

Also in Magnet books by the same author:

THE ADVENTURES OF ODD AND ELSEWHERE
THE SECRET OF THE SEVEN BRIGHT SHINERS
ODD AND THE GREAT BEAR

Other books about Odd and Elsewhere are:

THE RETURN OF THE GREAT BEAR
THE SECRET OF TIPPITY WITCHET
THE LOST TREASURE OF WALES

Published by Andre Deutsch

First published in Great Britain 1974
by Andre Deutsch Ltd, 105 Great Russell Street,
London WC1 as *Elsewhere and the Gathering of the Clowns*
Magnet paperback edition published 1982
by Methuen Children's Books Ltd,
11 New Fetter Lane, London EC4P 4EE
Copyright © 1974 by James Roose–Evans
Illustrations © 1974 by Brian Robb
All rights reserved
Printed in Great Britain by
Richard Clay (The Chaucer Press) Ltd,
Bungay, Suffolk

ISBN 0 416 25260 5

THIS THE FOURTH
OF
THE BOOKS OF ODD AND ELSEWHERE
AND
IT IS FOR THE CHILDREN
OF THE SOLIHULL PRIMARY SCHOOLS
WHO
FIRST
SANG
THE SONGS OF
ODD AND ELSEWHERE
ON
THE BOOK TRAIN
FROM
BIRMINGHAM
TO
THE CHILDREN'S BOOK SHOW IN LONDON
NOVEMBER 1972

Author's Note

TIPPITY-WITCHIT is a
variant of
TYPITY-WITCHET, the title of
a song made famous by
Joseph Grimaldi, the renowned
English clown.

Odd and Elsewhere were sitting on the steps of their gipsy caravan which stood among the apple trees on the lower lawn of Fenton House in Hampstead. The caravan had been given to them one Christmas by the King of the Clowns for the part they had played in helping to unmask a famous gang of thieves.

It was a spring day but so warm it felt like summer and holidays. Collander Moll, who was the house-keeper, had announced she was going to spring-clean and had shooed them both out of doors. So the two friends had decided that they would clean out their caravan.

'Oh, look!' said Odd suddenly, pointing towards the top of the old house. 'It's Collander Moll spring-cleaning the attics.'

From one of the small windows in the roof a mop shot out. It rotated vigorously and bits of fluff floated down like dirty snow. There also seemed to be lots of small squares of paper, of different colours, drifting down.

'Hey, that's my stamp collection!' cried Elsewhere,

jumping down from the caravan and racing up the steps to the upper lawn. At that moment Collander Moll appeared on the little square balcony that opened off the attic rooms in which Odd and Elsewhere lived.

'Those are my stamps you've just thrown out!' shouted Elsewhere.

'There's dirty bits of old paper,' came the reply. 'You don't want those!'

The two friends raced up the back stairs as fast as they could to see what else was being thrown away. It was always the same. The rest of the year Collander Moll lived in a muddle like a magpie's nest, but come spring-cleaning time and everything was thrown out. She was just as ruthless then with her own things as with everybody else's. Afterwards she would spend hours emptying the dust-bins in order to find her spare set of false teeth or Hallelujah's reading glasses. Hallelujah Jones, the gardener, was her father, and both of them worked for the National Trust which looks after historic old houses.

Dumped on the landing outside their room was a large pile of picture books, pine cones, feathers, old bottles dug up from the dump at the bottom of the garden, Elsewhere's conjuring tricks, his stamp album, and Odd's collection of honey jars. They could hear Collander Moll's broom going thud-thud-thud into the corners, while her duster went flip-flop-flap. They stood in the doorway of their room, aghast. Moll's damp face was speckled with dust and feathers, her eyes shining madly. They had never known her quite like this before. She laughed when she saw them, wiping her face in one of her dusters.

'The house is going to be re-decorated, look you, and

everything has to be cleared out of the way so as the men can get on with their work.'

'Does that mean we are going away?' asked Odd.

'You'd better find somewhere to put all that rubbish,' replied Collander Moll, ignoring his question. 'Else I'll get Hallelujah to burn it on his bonfire.'

'No!' protested Elsewhere. 'We'll carry it all down to our caravan.'

When everything had been stored away, Odd perched on the bunk at the far end of the caravan and clapped his paws.

'We're like a snail now,' he laughed. 'We can take our home with us wherever we go.'

Elsewhere looked at him thoughtfully. '*That* is an idea,' he murmured, leaning over the half door.

He looked out at the empty shafts of the caravan. 'Only we haven't got a horse,' he added.

'What *are* you talking about?' asked Odd, jumping down and joining him at the door.

'Don't you see?' explained Elsewhere excitedly. 'If we had a horse we could really move our house. And if we could move, then we could travel. And if we could travel, then we could go places!'

He turned to Odd, his yellow hair flying in all directions. 'We could be like real gipsies,' he said. 'We've got a stove to cook on, a bed to sleep in, a bucket to wash in. Only we haven't got a horse.'

'But do you know about horses?' asked Odd cautiously, feeling a little apprehensive. He knew, from past experience, how all too easily Elsewhere got carried away with new ideas.

'You just sit on the steps,' replied Elsewhere loftily, 'and hold the reins and say, gee-up!'

They were interrupted by Hallelujah calling to them. He was waving something in his hand.

'What is it, Hallelujah?' asked Elsewhere.

'It's for you, boy bach,' he replied, handing an impressive-looking envelope to him. Odd and Elsewhere stared at it. Neither of them had ever received a letter. It was addressed to:

Elsewhere,
c/o Fenton House,
(by arrangement with the National Trust)
Hampstead,
London,
Great Britain,
Europe,
The World,
Space.

'What does it say?' asked Odd, as Elsewhere opened it.

'It's from the King!' exclaimed Elsewhere.

'How can it be from the King?' said Hallelujah. 'We've only got a Queen.'

'It's from the King of the Clowns,' explained Elsewhere.

'Oh, *him*!' replied Hallelujah. 'And what is he wanting with you then?'

'There's to be a Gathering,' answered Elsewhere.

'What's a Gathering?' asked Odd.

'It's when the King summons all the clowns to assemble at Tippity House – that's where the King lives. This letter is an invitation to attend the Gathering of the Clowns at Tippity House.'

'When's it supposed to be then?' asked Hallelujah, gazing at him with a new interest.

Elsewhere looked at the letter. 'It's seven days from now,' he answered.

He stared at the empty shafts of the caravan which the King had given them. 'If only we had a horse,' he sighed, 'we could have gone in our caravan.'

It was at that moment they heard a familiar voice calling from the street, on the other side of the garden wall. 'Rag-a-bone! Any old iron! Rag-a-bone!' It was the scrap merchant on his rounds for any old iron or junk. Odd and Elsewhere at once raced down the garden path to greet him.

Outside the front gate stood the rag-and-bone man in a leather jerkin, the sleeves of his striped shirt rolled up above his hairy forearms, and a red and white hand-kerchief at his neck. 'Hallo there!' he grinned, pushing back his cap.

He climbed down from his cart and tethered the horse to the railings. Usually the cart was loaded with old iron bed-steads and park railings and gas cookers. Today it was empty except for a bundle of old clothes and some gas pipes. 'Ah, business is very poorly nowadays,' he grunted.

Collander Moll came bustling out, wiping her hands in her apron, but her damp face was still smudged with dust and feathers.

'Come you in then for a nice cup of tea and one of my Welsh cakes,' she burbled. 'I'm having a spring-clean, but there's always time for a cup of tea and a chat, look you!'

'That's right kind of you, lass,' answered the rag-and-bone man. 'I'll just give Tipsy her elevenses first.'

He slung a bag of oats round the neck of his horse, Tipsy-Gipsy, and then followed Collander Moll down the area steps into her kitchen.

Odd and Elsewhere stood staring at Tipsy who took

no notice of them; being blinkered she could only see what was in front of her.

'She's a small horse,' observed Elsewhere thoughtfully. 'She'd fit between the shafts of our caravan all right.'

'But we couldn't just take her!' protested Odd.

'No,' answered Elsewhere, 'but we could ask Mr Rag-Bone if Tipsy would like a holiday.'

When they put the idea to him, Mr Rag-Bone seemed very pleased. 'I was only thinking today,' he said, 'as to how I was going to have to let Tipsy go. It's not just that business ain't what it used to be, but you try driving a horse and cart through London today. It's worse than a blooming obstacle race. No. I've seen a little second-hand van that I've decided to invest in. So,' he paused, 'if you'd really like Tipsy then you can have her. I'll be glad to know she's got a good home. You'll be doing me a favour,' he added as they were about to protest.

He untethered Tipsy and led her towards the caravan.

'What are all those straps for?' asked Odd anxiously.

'That's her harness. You take it off at the end of the day and leave her free to graze. Then in the morning you give her some oats, strap her up, and she's ready for work. It's quite easy. This goes under here, those two over there, and you pull these in tight here, and then buckle these two straps. You'll soon get the knack of it.'

He gave Tipsy a light tap on the nose and she shot backwards into the shafts and was harnessed up.

There's not much to it,' he declared. 'You just give her nose a squeeze if she's any trouble. You'll soon get the hang of it.'

He picked up his bundle of rags and gas pipes.

'What about the cart?' asked Hallelujah.

'I know an antique dealer down the hill will buy that from me. I'll get him to come and take it away.'

'What about steering?' asked Odd, tugging at his sleeve.

'Oh, that's easy as riding a bicycle,' he laughed. 'Left rein to go left, right rein to go right. That's what they mean by the old expression, Right as Rein! Ta, now!'

And with that he was gone, almost as though he were afraid that they might suddenly change their minds.

Tipsy, stood, her bag of oats slung round her neck, quietly munching.

'She seems quiet enough,' observed Odd.

'She seems quiet enough,' said Odd. That was until they had got on to the motorway. Of course they ought never to have gone on it in the first place, but Elsewhere had insisted.

'It's so much quicker,' he had argued. 'The road goes straight almost all the way. We take the M6 past Birmingham, and then go on to the M5 to Worcester, and then on to the A44. I looked it up in Hallelujah's road map.'

Collander Moll had packed supplies of food, enough to feed an army for at least two weeks. It had been agreed that they would all meet up at Collander Moll's auntie's outside Llandrindod Wells.

'Dad and I will take a few days holiday once the men start work. So leave a message with auntie just to say where you are. And don't forget to remember us to Mr Goodman.' Mr Goodman was a friend of Odd and Elsewhere's who ran a butterfly farm in Radnorshire and since Tippity House was in the next county it had been decided they would also call on him and his friend Arbuthnot.

Now, as the cars thundered past at seventy miles an

hour, changing from lane to lane, Tipsy rolled her eyes and whinnied.

'Why is she foaming at the mouth?' asked Odd, holding on tightly to the reins, while Elsewhere sat on the roof above, watching the traffic go by.

'Oh, I expect she's eaten something that disagrees with her. I say, isn't this exciting! But I do wish Tipsy weren't so slow. It will take us simply ages to get there at this rate.'

Odd peered up at Elsewhere whose legs were dangling just above his head.

'She isn't a racehorse, you know,' he answered rather sharply.

He was beginning to feel a little disgruntled as well as nervous. It was just like Elsewhere to get them into a situation like this. He was always showing off and saying he knew all about things when really he knew nothing at all. Odd realised now that Elsewhere had never been on a motorway before, and he certainly did not know anything about horses, even if he had been used to living in a caravan as a clown.

They had not gone very far when there was a sound of screeching brakes.

'What is it?' asked Odd, who did not dare look round. He was holding on tightly to the reins because every time a lorry roared past, Tipsy always threatened to rear up. In fact Odd had the distinct impression that Tipsy would much rather go backwards than forwards.

Angry voices were now shouting.

'Get off the motorway, will you? Get that ruddy circus out of the way. Get on to the hard shoulder.'

Then, in unison, they chanted, '*Get on to the hard shoulder!*'

'What do they mean, the hard shoulder?' asked Odd.

'I don't know,' replied Elsewhere.

By now Tipsy had come to a standstill. She refused to go any farther. Peering round the side of the caravan, Odd could see a line of cars and lorries, nose to tail, their drivers honking their hooters, and shaking their fists. In the fast lane, on the far side, the motorists who were driving at seventy miles and more an hour turned startled glances as they raced past. 'Oh, my goodness, oh, my oddness!' cried Odd to himself. Already he could see the headlines in the newspapers, *Pile-up on the M6*.

'Oh, come on, Tipsy!' shouted Elsewhere impatiently, slithering down from the roof and grabbing the reins from Odd.

'Gee up!' he cried, giving Tipsy a slap on the flanks. Startled, Tipsy reared up and shot forward.

'Hurrah!' shouted Elsewhere. 'You see, she only needed some encouragement. Ride 'em, cowboy!'

Suddenly Tipsy swerved and went straight towards the grassy bank on the side of the motorway. There was a wild screeching of brakes from the cars and lorries behind; the caravan slewed round, and shuddered to a standstill. There was a crash of china and glass, the splintering sound of breaking timbers, and Elsewhere was catapulted through the air.

The next thing he heard, as he lay spread-eagled on the bank, was the siren of a police car. When he opened his eyes he saw two policemen looking down at him. Tipsy was calmly grazing on the bank but there was no sign of Odd. Elsewhere sat up suddenly.

'Where's Odd?' he asked.

He got up and limped his way over to the caravan. Odd lay sprawled in the entrance, a large sticky pool forming at the side of his head.

'He's not dead, is he?' asked Elsewhere in an awed voice, staring at the sticky pool, 'That's not his brains, is it?'

One of the policemen bent down and put a finger in the dark pool. He sniffed at his finger and then tasted it. 'That's all right,' he grinned, 'it's only honey. A

jar of honey must have got broken along with all the crockery.'

Odd, opening one eye, looked straight into the pool of honey. His nose twitched. It was like a dream, he thought, waking up to find yourself in a pool of honey.

He opened the other eye and saw Elsewhere and the two policemen.

'Oh, my goodness, oh, my oddness!' he murmured. 'Whatever now?'

Odd had given up saying *whatever next*? With Elsewhere you just had to be prepared for anything.

He sat up slowly, carefully moving his head from side to side. Next he lifted his arms up and down. Then he stood up. 'No bones broken!' he said, and began to do a little song and dance.

> *Teddy on the railway*
> *Picking up stones.*
> *Along came an engine*
> *And broke poor Teddy's bones.*
> *Oh, said Teddy,*
> *That's not fair!*
> *Pooh, said the engine driver,*
> *I don't care!*

One of the policemen took out a notebook and looked sternly at Odd.

'Well now, seeing as you are all of one piece, perhaps you would like to explain exactly what you are doing on the motorway with a horse and a caravan? Can't you read?'

'Not very well,' replied Odd cheerfully.

'There is a large notice at the start of the motorway,' continued the policeman, 'which says very plainly, in large letters, *No learners, mopeds, invalid cars, pedestrians – or ANIMALS*, are allowed on the motorway!'

Odd went on singing to himself. He thought it only right that Elsewhere should answer. Besides, he was always so much better at wriggling his way out of awkward situations. A clown was as good as an actor, if not better, and Elsewhere was a very good clown. He could act or clown his way out of most things. And in no time at all Elsewhere had both policemen roaring with laughter as he mimed what had happened. They slapped him on the back and Elsewhere doubled up and rolled over so that they laughed even more.

'He's a real clown, ain't he!' said one.

'You can say that again!' laughed the other.

'Well now,' they said together, suddenly straightening their faces and trying to look like proper policemen, 'you just carry on along this hard shoulder, as it's called, until you come to the next exit. You won't meet any traffic on the hard shoulder unless it's a car that's broken down; in that case you'll have to wait until it's mended and moves back on to the motorway.'

'And remember,' added the second policeman, 'that on the A44 horses are still allowed the right of way over cars. That's the law. So even if they do honk their hooters you take no notice of them. Understand? But if you take my advice you'll try and get an early start each day when there's less traffic on the roads. But don't ride her uphill. Always get off when you come to a hill, and walk the horse. The same applies when you go down a hill. A horse isn't like a car. A horse is more like a human. You have to give it some thought.'

Wishing them good luck for the rest of their trip, the

25

two policemen climbed back into their white car with its winking blue light on top, and drove off.

As soon as they had cleared up the mess inside the caravan, the two friends set off, travelling along the hard shoulder.

'It's like having a road all to one's self!' laughed Odd.

Soon they came to a large sign indicating the exit from the motorway and they were on the A44 to Warwickshire and Worcestershire and Radnorshire.

As they travelled along, Elsewhere made up a song for Odd.

> *Teddy on the motorway*
> *With Tipsy on the trot.*
> *Along came a lorry*
> *And broke poor Teddy's honey-pot!*
> *Oh, said Teddy,*
> *That's not fair.*
> *Pooh! said the lorry driver,*
> *I don't care!*

The next morning, as soon as Tipsy had had her breakfast of oats, she was harnessed and led out on to the main road. The bells on her harness tinkled and her hooves went clip-clop. Elsewhere took the reins whilst Odd cooked their breakfast over the tiny stove. Elsewhere had found some mushrooms and Odd was frying these with some bread. The first person they met on the road was the postman.

'What's the road like ahead?' they asked.

'Oh, you be downhill all the way for the next three miles, and then you're on the flat for a goodish way. But you've got a nasty hill outside Burleston.'

They thanked the postman and the caravan rumbled on its way.

Down a side lane ran small, wide-awake children, their almost empty satchels bouncing. They were followed by older sisters with long hair like tents, still sleepy-eyed; and their older brothers, also with long hair, arguing and fighting, their satchels heavy and bulging with books. The small children jumped up and down with excitement when they saw the caravan, but their older sisters merely yawned and said, 'What's that then?', while their older brothers argued.

'It's gipsies,' said one.

'No, it ain't then!' said another.

'How much you bet then?'

Odd and Elsewhere left them waiting by the bus stop, still arguing. When they finally came to the hill the

postman had told them about, Elsewhere jumped down
and led Tipsy by the reins. Odd walked at the back,
ready to shove a piece of wood under the wheels if the
caravan should roll suddenly backwards.

It was when they got to the top of the hill that the
trouble started. Odd had been enjoying the slow pace of

the caravan, especially when he was holding the reins, because then he was on a level with the tops of hedges and could see over into the fields on either side. But Elsewhere was getting restless. It was not just that the novelty had worn off and he was now bored and wanting to be doing something different.

'We'll never get there at this rate!' he burst out suddenly. 'And then I'll be late for the Gathering.'

They had just reached the top of the hill when Elsewhere jumped up into the driver's seat, tugged at the reins, slapping Tipsy on the flanks with them, and set her off galloping downhill. Odd managed just in time to scramble on board.

'Oh, no, no, no!' he shouted, trying to stop Elsewhere. 'You mustn't – remember what the policeman told us!'

'Oh, bother the police!' replied Elsewhere. 'They are always fussing and saying you can't do this and you can't do that. Nonsense. You can see for yourself Tipsy's enjoying herself!'

Faster and faster galloped Tipsy, her mane flying out behind her, while all the pots and pans inside the caravan rattled and banged.

'But don't you see,' shouted Odd, 'she's only going so fast because of the weight of the caravan behind her. If she were to stop now, on this hill, the shafts would snap!'

He struggled and fought with Elsewhere. Any moment they might have another accident and this time they might not be so lucky. With one paw he aimed a blow at Elsewhere's head, knocking him off-balance. At the same time Odd wound the reins about his paws and began to tug. Fortunately, the road now straightened out, so that Tipsy and the caravan were

able to slow down. Sweat was pouring down Tipsy's
flanks which heaved like bellows, and saliva streamed
from her jaws. Odd was crying with pain because the
reins had twisted so tightly round his paws. Elsewhere
slumped back in a deep sulk. Neither of them spoke
for a long time.

Then Elsewhere let out a deep sigh. 'I'm sorry, Odd,'
he said. 'But it's so important I get there in time. You
see, a Gathering is something very special. It happens
perhaps only once in a lifetime, and when it does every
clown is expected to leave whatever he is doing and go
at once to Tippity House. It's a matter of honour. I
must get there!'

31

There were tears in his eyes. Odd had not realised until now just how important the Gathering was to Elsewhere.

'You see,' he continued, 'every clown dreams of being able to visit Tippity House at least once in his life. But you have to wait until the King invites you. It's something very special. You can't just walk up to the front door and ring the bell and say, Can I see the King? He probably wouldn't be there anyway, because most of the year he's off round the world, visiting clowns in Germany and Japan and America and places like that.'

'And Wales,' added Odd, remembering the one time that he and Elsewhere had met him.

'And Wales!' laughed Elsewhere.

'*And* it was the King that gave us this caravan.'

'Yes, I know,' answered Elsewhere. 'And that was why I was anxious to arrive in it. Just to show that we really had used it. But even if Tipsy were a racehorse, which she isn't; and even if it were flat all the way, which it isn't; and even if there were no other traffic on the road, we still wouldn't get there in time for the Gathering. And we've lost three days already.'

By now they were back on the road and approaching a crossroads with many signposts pointing in different directions.

Odd reined in at the side of the road. He looked at Elsewhere and said, 'Why don't you hitch-hike? After all, if I can hitch-hike, which I did when I was searching for the Great Bear, then you ought to be able to. All you have to do is hold out your paw, oh sorry!' he grinned. 'I mean your hand.'

'What about Tipsy and the caravan?' asked Elsewhere.

'That's all right. I can manage her now,' replied Odd. 'You don't have to worry about me.'

'Will you follow on?'

'No, I'll make my way to the Granary and stay with Mr Goodman and Arbuthnot. I'll wait for you there.'

Elsewhere gave Odd a hug and then jumped down on the roadside. He waited until the caravan was out of sight, then set off in the direction of the motorway. There seemed to be a lot of traffic on the road. Brightly coloured sports cars whizzed past, lorries and trucks roared by. In no time at all, he thought, one would stop for him, and then he would really be on his way. He began to feel much more cheerful as he strode along. He started to sing and the song he sang was the Song of the Clown.

> *When you're up, you're up,*
> *And when you're down, you're down,*
> *That's what it is to be a clown.*
> *Now up! Now down!*
> *Uppity-up and downity-down!*
> *That's what it is to be a clown!*

Three hours later Elsewhere was still on the road. Cars and lorries whizzed past but none of them stopped. It was raining, and every time a car drove through a puddle Elsewhere was drenched all down one side. As he limped along, footsore and damp, he could not help wishing that he had stayed with Odd. When the sun came out, however, he began to cheer up. He sang a song to keep his spirits up. It was a song with actions.

> *Eeskie-weeskie spider,*
> *Climbing up the spout –*

He placed his right thumb against the first finger of his left hand, then moved the first finger of the right hand up to meet the left thumb, and so over and over, up and up, till his hands were above his head.

> *Down came the rain*
> *And washed poor Eeskie out –*

Here he beat a tattoo on his chest like the sound of rain drumming on a roof –

> *Out came the sun*
> *And dried up all the rain –*

He opened wide his arms –

> *Eeskie-weeskie spider*
> *Climbing up again.*

And here he repeated the gesture of thumb on finger, over and over.

Suddenly a car drew up and a man leaned his head out of the window. Elsewhere ran across to him with great excitement.

'Are you advertising something?' asked the man.

'No,' replied Elsewhere, puzzled. Then, before he could ask the man where he was going, the car drove off.

Now it was getting dark and lights in houses were being switched on. He knew that once it was really dark his chances of getting a lift would be gone and another day wasted.

Just beyond a roundabout he came to a workmen's café, set back from the road with petrol pumps and a garage. Several lorries were drawn up. Peering through the dirty net curtains of the café windows he could see the drivers of the lorries sitting at linoleum-covered tables, eating platefuls of bacon, eggs and chips, sipping hot sweet tea from cracked mugs and reading the football results. Elsewhere pressed his nose against the window, wondering what to do. It was raining again and the raindrops slid down the window-panes, wetting his face. He looked round and noticed that one of the lorries was open at the back. On the side of the van were painted the words, FROM TOTNESS TO TIPPERARY – REMOVALS. In the dusk it looked like – Tippity, and that

comforted him. I'll shelter there, he thought, then when the driver comes out I'll ask him which way he is going, and perhaps he'll give me a lift.

The inside of the van was high and dark, crowded with furniture like an auction hall. Elsewhere curled up in an armchair, between a grandfather clock, a large birdcage, and a heavy wardrobe with a long mirror on its front. Dimly he could see himself reflected. It was warm and dry inside the van. He snuggled down to wait. The rain drummed on the roof, a steady soothing sound.

When Elsewhere awoke it was so dark he could not even see his reflection in the tall mirror. He sat up with a start. For a moment he could not remember where he was. He listened to a creaking sound, like that of an old sailing ship at sea in a storm. Then he realised that the van was in motion, travelling fast. He had no idea how long he had been asleep or where they now were. In a panic he fought his way to the back of the van. Feeling his way in the dark, he climbed to the top of a chest of drawers when suddenly he was thrown forward as, abruptly, the lorry changed gear. He lay sprawling between a settee and a rocking-horse. It was like an obstacle race, he thought, only an obstacle race in which you were also blindfolded.

The doors of the van were now closed but he could feel a draught coming from high up and he discovered that one of the upper doors was slightly ajar. Peering out he could see a paleness in the sky, but whether it was the paleness of dawn or dusk he could not tell. The road unrolled swiftly behind the van, like a bale of cloth, across miles and miles of open moorland. He sniffed. He felt sure he could smell something salt in the air. Now it was getting lighter which must mean, he thought, that it was dawn. He must have slept all night in the van – in which case he had lost another day. Of course, it all depended in which direction the van was travelling. The important thing, therefore, was to find out from the driver where they were.

He made his way towards the front of the van, where there would be a window or an opening of some kind into the driver's cabin. Up and down he slithered, 'That's what it is to be a clown!' he muttered to himself, 'now up, now down.' He was bruised all over, his shirt torn; and he was very winded by the time he got to the front of the van.

'Oh, no!' he cried. For there was nothing but a solid wooden wall. He put his ear to it and, above the noise of the engine, could hear the murmur of voices, the driver talking to his mate.

He knocked with his gloved hand on the partition. But there was no answer. He banged. Nothing happened. He kicked. But they could not hear him. He sat, perched on a mangle, wondering what next he should do.

The smell of salt was stronger now. If it was the sea then it could only mean he was miles off track. Tippity

37

House was in the middle of England, nowhere near the sea.

'I've got to stop the driver!' he said, gazing up at the roof as though in search of inspiration.

'But, of course!' he exclaimed suddenly. 'Of course!'

Recklessly jumping across ravines of furniture, clambering over towers of packing boxes, he made his way back to the crack between the two upper doors of the van. Carefully he eased his way out and climbed up on to the roof. The wind up there blew so strong that he had to shove his cap in his pocket. Ahead of him stretched a smooth surface with no footholds or hand grips. Inch by inch he wriggled forward; once he got to the front, he thought, he would be able to lean over and catch the driver's attention.

Suddenly the angle of the roof seemed to change. One moment it had been horizontal and now it was tilting as the van slowly drove uphill. Just as Elsewhere was convinced he was about to slide off backwards, the angle of the van changed as it came to the top of the hill. He sighed with relief as once again the roof levelled and he could inch forward a little nearer to the front. Then, to his horror, the roof began to tilt again, but this time forwards. He realised the van was now going downhill. The tilt of the roof got steeper and steeper and the van, rapidly gathering speed, went faster and faster. Suddenly Elsewhere slid straight across the shiny surface. He closed his eyes and held his breath, hoping it would all be over very quickly.

He was saved by a rim at the front of the van, jutting up about an inch. For a moment he lay there, hardly daring to believe his good fortune. Then, carefully, he leaned over and tapped on the window screen below.

'D'you hear that, Fred?' said the driver's mate.

'What's that then, Bill?' answered the driver, peering with sleepy, blood-shot eyes at the road ahead.

'D'you hear that tapping?'

'What tapping?'

'There!'

'Sounds like a bird then, don't it?'

'A bird?'

'Yer, seagull I expect.'

'A seagull wouldn't ruddy tap at the window!' exclaimed Bill. 'Now would it?'

'Well, it might if it needed something,' replied Fred.

'Don't be daft!'

Elsewhere sighed. He did not seem to be having much luck. Wedging one foot behind the rim of the roof, he slowly lowered himself over so that he was hanging upside down over the windscreen and waving his cap.

'Blimey!' said Bill. 'Look up there, mate. It's a ruddy clown!'

'What you playing at, Bill? You trying to make me have an accident. What you mean – a clown? It's you that's a silly clown!'

'Up there, Fred. Can't yer see?'

Fred looked up for a moment. 'Cor!' he gasped. 'How'd he get up there, I wonder?'

'Must have flown,' answered Bill.

'Clowns don't fly!'

'Perhaps he's a flying clown,' suggested Bill.

'Funny, ain't it?' chuckled Fred.

Suddenly Elsewhere's foot was dislodged and he fell on to the bonnet of the van. He sat there, dirty, bedraggled, bruised, staring straight into Fred's face.

'D'you think he's broke a leg?' asked Bill.

'Better stop then, hadn't we?' replied Fred, slowing down.

And so, at last, the van drew up and Elsewhere told them how he had come to be on top of their van.

'I thought I heard something knocking in the night,' said Bill.

'He thought it was bats had got in the van,' laughed Fred.

'Where are you supposed to be going then?' asked Bill.

'To Tippity House.'

'Where's that then?'

'It's in Shropshire.'

'Cor, blimey! You know where you are now, don't you?'

'No. Where?' asked Elsewhere.

'You're in Aberdeen. In the far north of Scotland. Can't you smell them kippers?'

The removal men had given Elsewhere a big breakfast in a workmen's café down on the quayside at Aberdeen, among the old warehouses and fishermen's cottages. Then Fred introduced him to a red-faced, ginger-haired, giant of a man.

'This is Hamish McTavish,' he announced. 'He's driving a load of kippers to Edinburgh. He'll give you a lift that far. From there you'll have to make your own way over the border to Carlisle and down to Crewe.'

Elsewhere who had been studying a map looked up. 'I'll never make it in the time!' he said. 'I've only got three days left, and it's about four hundred miles!'

'There's no such thing as never,' growled Hamish, glowering at him. 'Hae ye no heard of Bruce and the spider?'

'No. What did he do?'

'He wae King o' Scotland lang since. One day he wae hiding in a barn from his enemies. And he noticed this wee spider, hanging from its web. He watched it trying to swing from one beam tae another. It took his mind off his own worries to watch it. Six times that wee spider tried to get across. And Robert Bruce swore that if it succeeded the seventh time, then he would follow its example, he'd take heart, and try once more against the English. This was way back in 1314, the year of the famous Battle of Bannockburn. Nae doubt ye've heard o' that?'

Hamish was so fierce that Elsewhere did not dare say he had not, so he nodded eagerly.

'Well, then, when the wee spider finally got across, Robert Bruce said to himself, "If at first ye don't succeed, then try, try again!" And that's exactly what he did. So don't you be telling me it's impossible. I'll get ye to Edinburgh and you'll see what happens after that.

And now, if you've finished wasting time grumbling, we'll be on our way!'

So Elsewhere thanked the removal men and climbed up into the seat next to Hamish. They drove along the coast, through Dundee – 'where they make cake and marmalade,' said Hamish – over the Firth of Forth, and down into Edinburgh.

'There, man! There's a quarter of your journey completed!' grinned Hamish. 'Now if you nip across Princes Street, towards the Castle, you'll come to Waverley Station. With luck you should catch the next train for Carlisle and Crewe.'

Elsewhere was about to protest and say he had no money for trains when Hamish winked and added, 'I don't think the lack of a ticket will stop the likes of you! But remember, if at first you don't succeed . . . .'

'Try, try again!' laughed Elsewhere. 'And thank you!'

He wandered on to the main platform and looked up at the indicator board. Hamish had been right. There was a train, leaving in fifteen minutes, for Carlisle and Crewe. The first thing was to get past the guard at the ticket barrier.

The great advantage of being small is that you can slip past people without their always noticing you. Elsewhere waited until he saw a man and his large wife, with lots of luggage, going through the barrier, and under cover of their suitcases, he slipped past without any difficulty.

The next problem was to decide where to hide on the train when the ticket inspector came through. On a large crate he noticed several labels addressed to a big store in Crewe. He removed one of these and tied it on his arm. If the guard discovered him he would just lie still and pretend to be part of the luggage.

The mailbags were like lumpy mattresses, but even though they were so uncomfortable he soon fell fast asleep. He awoke to find the train pulling into a station.

'Carlisle! This is Carlisle station!' came a posh voice over the loudspeaker. 'All change here. We regret that owing to weather conditions the trains to Crewe are cancelled.'

The guard lowered the window and leaned out.

'What's happening?' Elsewhere heard him ask.

'Line's blocked with snow,' came the reply.

Doors were opening and there was a babble of voices. Elsewhere slipped out easily without being seen. Once outside the station he paused to get his bearings. He knew that he had to travel south and from the map he remembered that this would take him through the Lake District. The snow was falling steadily. How far he would get he did not know. The important thing was to keep moving. He thought of Bruce and the spider and trudged on through the thickening snow.

He could hardly believe it when a motor-bike stopped and the young driver yelled, 'Would you like a lift? I'm going as far as Bolton, if I can make it, that is.'

Elsewhere climbed on the back and placed his arms round the young man's waist. The bike revved and roared, and then with a slither half-way across the road, was off. In the end Elsewhere did not have to hold on because the ice on his hands froze fast to the driver's coat.

So, by means of a mail van, a milk cart, an ambulance, and a school bus, Elsewhere got to within a hundred miles of Tippity House. It was the final day. He had

travelled out of the snow and wintry weather into a mild, spring-like day, with daffodils and primroses in flower. He looked more like a tramp than a clown and he was limping badly. He had been on the road for more than two hours and was beginning to worry lest, having got so near, he would not now make it in time. He plodded on.

Clip-clop! Clip-clop! he could hear a horse and wagon approaching from behind. For one wild moment he thought that perhaps it was Odd come in search of him. But the hooves were heavier than those of Tipsy. He was too tired to look round. Then he heard someone shouting at him; so at last he stopped and turned.

A boy was waving at him from an empty hay wagon drawn by a grey and white cart-horse. At his side was a girl in a long striped dress with a bonnet on her head. Both had black hair, turned-up noses, and bright red patches on their cheeks.

47

'Whoa there!' The boy pulled hard on the reins and the cart came to a standstill.

'Jump on!' he called out.

'Where are you going?'

'To the Gathering, of course?'

Elsewhere stared at him. 'What Gathering?' he said.

'The Gathering of the Clowns, of course. That's why I called out to you. Aren't you going there?'

Elsewhere climbed up into the wagon and perched on the side rail.

'My name's Wiggie,' said the boy. 'You know – "'Ere we go!"' He laughed. Then Elsewhere introduced himself.

'This is my sister, Bloggs,' said Wiggie. Elsewhere shook hands.

'Why is she called Bloggs?' he asked.

'No one knows, do they, Bloggs? Bloggs is Bloggs and

48

no questions asked. That's right, ain't it, Bloggs?' said Wiggie, cracking his whip. Bloggs blushed and giggled.

The cart rolled along, the big wheels spinning like plates.

'Bloggs doesn't say much, does Bloggs?' he added. 'But she's a great cook, ain't you, Bloggs? You wait till you taste her Tippity Pudding. That's why she's coming along. The King says no one knows how to make Tippity Pudding like Bloggs.'

'What do you do then?' asked Elsewhere, staring at Wiggie's knicker-bocker suit, the corduroy cap on his head, and the satchel slung round his neck.

'I look after the horses.'

'Why do you need such a big cart?'

'Because we shall be picking up other clowns on the way, that's why. There hasn't been a Gathering like this for years. Our Dad's Dad used to tell us of a Gathering when he was a boy. That was when the last King retired. A Gathering only happens when the King is going to retire. The King calls together all the clowns from all over the world to assemble at Tippity House. For two days everyone dances and sings and entertains the King. He watches them all perform, one after the other, to see which is the best clown. But it remains a secret between the King and the clown he has chosen. Only when the King officially retires does he announce to all the clowns in the world the name of his successor.'

As they were talking, they came to a roundabout and there on the roadside were three clowns with bundles and suitcases. One was throwing apples in the air, the second was catching them, and the third – was eating them! They cheered when they saw Wiggie's cart and, throwing their bags over the rail, climbed on board.

49

'Whizz, Tizz, and Phizz!' they announced, staring at Elsewhere.

'Which is which?' he asked.

'We answer to any name!' they replied, and fell about laughing.

'And you?' they asked.

'I'm Elsewhere.'

They clicked their heels and bowed; then all three simultaneously shook Elsewhere by the hand. Suddenly, without any warning, they had thrown him up into the air.

When they reached the next town there were more clowns lined up on the side of the road. Some carried flags on their luggage so that you could tell which country they came from, Sweden, Germany, Denmark, Finland, Norway, Russia, China, Japan, America, Brazil, Sierra Leone, Mexico, the Seychelles, Jamaica, Uruguay, Australia, New Zealand, and many other places. Soon the cart was crammed with clowns forming a pyramid with Whizz, Tizz and Phizz at the top. They all chattered away as noisily as rooks at dusk. The many bright colours of their costumes made the wagon look like a float at a carnival. Crowds in the streets, people at their bedroom windows, men on rooftops replacing slates, farmers on tractors ploughing fields, all cheered and waved as the cart went by. Juggling apples, blowing trumpets, beating drums, shaking tambourines, the pyramid of clowns travelled on its way, with Bloggs up front silent, red-faced and giggling, and Wiggie shouting out, 'Gee up, 'ere we go!'

It was all so exciting, exactly like the old days, that suddenly Elsewhere wished that Odd were there to share it with him. How he would have enjoyed it.

Gradually they met up with other carts, wagons, and caravans, all crowded with clowns. They also passed clowns on cycles – tandems, penny-farthings, ordinary bicycles, and tricycles; there was even one clown pedalling away like a madman on a cycle with only one wheel.

All the carts and caravans and bicycles, tricycles and unicycles converged at the entrance to a long drive that led to an old house standing in parkland, among ancient oaks and beeches, with sheep grazing. This was Tippity House, the home of the King of the Clowns.

The house was a square shape of red brick with a large door in the centre and many tall windows to each side and above. In front was a circular lawn so that the drive went all the way round. At every window, looking out and waving to the new arrivals, were yet more clowns. And there, standing at the top of the steps, waiting to greet them, was the King himself. His costume was like that of the other clowns, only more magnificent. His hair was as yellow as Elsewhere's, but more golden. He looked as old as the oldest clown and as young as the youngest. You knew, before you had said anything, that he understood all your problems and that there was nothing you could not tell him. Above all, he possessed the secret of Tippity-Witchit, the secret that only the King knew and which had been handed down since the time of Joseph Grimaldi, the greatest of all British clowns, who had invented it.

'Welcome, welcome!' he cried, greeting each new arrival by name. As soon as he saw Elsewhere, in spite of his tattered appearance, he knew who he was, and he asked after Odd, and Collander Moll (*and* her auntie), Hallelujah, Mr Goodman 'and his friend with the funny name, Arbuthnot!' He asked if Elsewhere and Odd had used the caravan he had given them. So Elsewhere explained, and the King nodded and smiled as though he understood all about it.

Suddenly everyone stopped talking. Along the drive, silently except for the crunch of wheels on gravel, glided

a magnificent car, a large silver Renault with a long
sloping bonnet and gold headlamps. Seated at the
wheel was a slim figure, dressed in a white suit, white
gloves, a white cap with a large peak, and wearing
goggles against the glare of the setting sun. The car
drew up at the foot of the steps and the driver got out.

He bounded up the steps, removing his goggles. He bowed low before the King and they shook hands, his dark eyes twinkling.

'Who is that?' whispered Elsewhere to one of the clowns next to him.

'That? Oh, that is Coco, the French clown.'

Up and down the corridors of Tippity House and inside every room there was a hum and buzz of voices; it sounded exactly like being inside a beehive. Clowns were busy making themselves known to each other, exchanging news and stories, while bets were being placed as to who was most likely to become King of the Clowns. The popular choice seemed to be Coco, the French clown. Almost everyone agreed that he was the most famous. And that night, at dinner, it was observed that the King had placed Coco in the seat of honour, next to himself.

They all sat at a long table lit by many candles. They had a lot to eat and each course was made from a different national recipe. They had a Danish hors d'oeuvre to begin with, followed by a fish dish cooked according to a French recipe; then Boeuf à la Strogonoff, from a Russian recipe. The last dish of all was Bloggs' Tippity Pudding served in large bowls. You dipped in a spoon and helped yourself and came back for more. It seemed never to come to an end and it tasted of plump juicy blackberries and crunchy hazelnuts; of walnuts, raisins, and sultanas soaked in brandy; with crumbled fruit cake soaked in sherry; and cool sliced pears set in a firm yellowy custard, sprinkled with grated coconut. On top of it all was poured a thick cream flecked with grated orange peel.

Elsewhere noticed how, when they were eating
Bloggs' Tippity Pudding, there was silence at the table.
Everyone had at least two helpings and scraped the
bowls and licked their spoons.

'You've done us proud again, Bloggs!' said the King,

and Bloggs, blushing and giggling, dropped a curtsey.

Afterwards there were crackers to pull, like at Christmas, and every clown found inside a motto that suited him. Elsewhere's was *Aim high – there is plenty of room to fall.* He did not like the sound of that at all. Did it mean that he did not stand a chance and that he were better not to try? But if that were the case, why aim high in the first place? He was still trying to puzzle this out when the King rose to make a speech. He welcomed them all to Tippity House and said that the time was approaching when he must retire, and that therefore it was now his task to choose a successor.

'Tomorrow will be free for each clown to rehearse. Then, in the evening, in the Big Top, which is in the meadow at the back of the house, the Entertainment will commence, and it will continue for two days. Every clown will perform twice, tomorrow and the day after. Only when I have seen every clown perform twice shall I decide who is to be the next King of the Clowns.'

Everyone applauded. Coco rose and, lifting his glass, proposed a toast to the King. Everyone stood up and cried out with a great shout – THE KING. Then they sat down again, laughing and talking. Elsewhere could hear the King roaring with laughter at Coco's stories. Coco's dark eyes flashed, and his hands darted like white butterflies as he mimed and acted the stories. Suddenly Elsewhere felt very jealous. Suddenly he wanted very much to be King. He had never really thought about it before because the King had always been king for as long as he could remember. There had never been any thought about anyone else being King. But now that the King had announced his impending retirement it was a different matter. Elsewhere thought what fun it would be to ride at the head of the procession, to have lots of new clothes; and to be the centre of attention.

There was an especially loud burst of laughter from the King's end of the table and, looking up, Elsewhere saw that the King was asking Coco to repeat one of his stories so that everyone could enjoy it. Soon Coco had the whole table spellbound and Elsewhere thought. What chance do I stand?

'But if Coco is so popular,' he said afterwards to Whizz, Tizz and Phizz who shared the room next to his, 'and the King thinks so highly of him, what is the point of gathering us all together and having the Entertainment?'

'Because,' answered Whizz, 'there's many a slip,'

'Twixt the cup,' added Phizz,

'And the lip,' completed Tizz; then all three added with a grin, 'an old English proverb!'

'You see,' continued Whizz, swinging from the top of the four-poster in Elsewhere's bedroom, 'there's always new clowns coming up, clowns whose work the King doesn't know. So it's quite possible for a complete outsider to be named. That's what happened to the present King; practically no one had heard of him at the time. So, you see, we all stand a chance, and that's what makes it all so exciting! Any one of us could become King.'

'Any one of us could become King,' chorused Whizz, Tizz and Phizz in unison.

Elsewhere laughed. 'What would happen,' he asked, 'if one of *you* became King?'

'Why,' said Whizz,

'Don't you see,' said Tizz,

'We'd all three have to be King!' said Phizz. 'We'd be known as King Whizz-Tizz-Phizz!'

They ran off to join a party of clowns who were going to take a look at the practice ring in the Big Top where they would have to perform the next day. But Elsewhere sat on alone, in his room, chewing the ends of his gloves, and worrying. Looking up, he observed his reflection in the window. Until then he had not realised how strange he must appear. His clothes were now torn, stained and dirty, while his hair stuck up all over the place.

'I look more like a scarecrow than a clown,' he murmured to himself. 'Oh, what am I going to do?'

Clip-clop went Tipsy's hooves along the lonely mountain lanes, while the old wheels of the caravan rumbled and grumbled. Odd had fallen asleep at the reins. He had taken the road from Knighton, past Bleddfa and its village school, where the children waved as he went past, Dolau, and Pen-y-Bont, as far as Llandrindod Wells, but it was on the other side of the town that he had lost his way. There were few houses in sight, and the lanes twisted, winding backwards and forwards like a tangled skein of wool. The few signposts seemed uncertain in which direction they ought to be pointing.

Suddenly Odd awoke. The setting sun through the hedgerows was pink and golden, the colour of honeysuckle. The narrow lane was banked high with cow parsley. Over a hedge came a cloud of yellow butterflies which fluttered round him, tickling his ears so that he giggled. Then they flew on down the lane, rising and falling, almost as though they were beckoning and leading the way.

'Oh, my goodness, oh, my oddness!' murmured Odd

to himself. Hearing his voice, Tipsy's ears stretched back as though trying to catch what he was saying.

'Oh, Tipsy!' he cried. 'I do believe we have got there after all!'

And there indeed, at the end of the lane, was the five-barred gate leading to the Granary, but now it had been repaired and repainted. And at the side was a splendid sign announcing

BUTTERFLY FARM
Granary Products Ltd.

The yellow brimstones led the way along the drive, exactly as they had done the first time Odd and Elsewhere had come to the Granary. Blackbirds again flew

up with loud warning chink-chinkchinks, and wood-pigeons, startled, banged their wings like wooden clappers.

'Goodness, what a noise!' laughed Odd. Then they had turned the corner and there was the old house with its clematis and wisteria, and the ship's bell above the door. Across the lawn a large, portly gentleman with several chins, was advancing, butterflies circling round his head.

'Oh, Mr Goodman!' cried Odd, running to meet him. Tipsy neighed and Odd, turning back, introduced them. The front door opened and a tiny man, smaller than Odd, emerged.

'Arbuthnot, isn't this a surprise!' laughed Odd.

In no time at all they had got Tipsy out of her harness, brushed and groomed her, and settled her in a stall.

'What are all these new buildings for?' asked Odd, as they came out of the dusty gloom of the stables. He was pointing to rows of brand new barns and outhouses.

'They are all part of our new enterprise,' answered Mr Goodman. 'We not only breed butterflies and moths but we now have a herd of dairy cows and we produce our own butter and cheese which we market. We've also got our own hens. Oh, and Arbuthnot has gone in for beekeeping, so we also make our own honey.'

'Yes, we've even named a honey after you!' laughed Arbuthnot. 'It's called Odd's Own Honey. It's very popular. You must taste it and tell us what you think.'

'Oh, yes, please!' laughed Odd, jumping up and down. Everywhere there was so much activity. 'Sometimes

it seems more like a factory here than a farm,' laughed Mr Goodman. 'But we have lots of young people who offer to come and help, or who want to stay and train for the work. There aren't enough beds for everyone but they don't seem to mind. They bring their tents or sleeping-bags and everyone takes a turn with the cooking or washing up. It's amazing how this old place has come alive!'

They were walking past the new cowsheds and Odd could hear, inside, the hum of the milking machines. Suddenly he heard another sound, coming across the meadow from behind a clump of trees.

'Someone's playing a guitar,' he observed.

'Yes, that's where the young people have pitched their

tents. Most of them have gone off for the weekend to a pop festival in Knighton,' explained Mr Goodman.

'Except for Sarah and Rufus,' added Arbuthnot, 'they have stayed behind to look after the small children.'

'Are they hippies?' asked Odd.

'I don't really know what a hippie is,' replied Mr Goodman. 'I think they are just themselves.'

By now the sun was beginning to set.

'Let's have our supper out of doors,' suggested Mr Goodman. 'It's a little early in the year but if we wrap up in blankets we shall be all right.'

Arbuthnot produced a long taper on the end of a stick and with this he went round lighting the night lights in Japanese lanterns which hung among the apple trees on the lawn.

There they sat talking until the last honeyed crumb was finished, and Odd lay back in his chair, licking his sticky paws. He told them how he and Elsewhere had set off on their journey to Tippity House; of their adventures on the motorway; and how Elsewhere had decided to go off on his own.

'One needs to go off on one's own every now and then,' observed Mr Goodman. 'I think it wasn't just that Elsewhere was afraid he might not get there in time. I have a feeling it was more than that.'

Inside the Granary oil lamps were being lit. Moths bumped against the Japanese lanterns, while in the woods behind they could hear owls hooting. Suddenly the telephone was ringing, stridently on the night air.

'Will you answer it, Arbuthnot?' said Mr Goodman. The clocks inside the house began to chime. He took out from his waistcoat pocket a gold watch. He opened the lid and checked the time.

'My father gave this to me,' he said. 'And his father gave it to him. And so on back through many generations. It's like this place, it's always been home to me, wherever I have been. When you have a home it doesn't really matter where you are, for it is always with you.'

Suddenly Arbuthnot was calling.

'Odd! It's for you. Can you come quickly? It's Elsewhere. He wants to speak to you urgently!'

Elsewhere was waiting for Odd at the main gates with a tricycle. Tippity House had proved to be much nearer to the Granary than they had realised, so that Arbuthnot had been able to drive Odd over first thing the next morning. 'Hop on!' said Elsewhere, 'and I'll tell you what it's all about.'

He talked so fast as he pedalled along, and the wind kept blowing his hair in Odd's face, that Odd had great difficulty in hearing half of what Elsewhere was saying. But he gathered that after the King's speech at dinner, Elsewhere had suddenly realised how out of practice he was, and that he no longer had a proper act to perform.

'And besides,' he added, 'for a good act you have to have an assistant. And *that*,' he concluded with a flourish, 'is where you come in!'

They parked the tricycle at the back of the house.

'I've got everything I need,' said Elsewhere, 'except for a large mirror.'

'What do you need a mirror for?' asked Odd.

'For a vanishing trick, that's what. It's a new idea I've had.'

They asked everybody where they could find a spare mirror. Finally one of the women from the village who was doing the bedrooms said, 'Have you looked in the attics? There's a lot of rubbish up there.'

So they climbed up and up until they came to many small rooms with sloping ceilings, each opening off the other, the whole length of the house. There were trunks full of old clothes smelling of mothballs, stuffed birds in glass domes, boxes of books all bound in mouldering leather, an Elizabethan chess table with a set of ivory men, drawers full of mouse-nibbled apples, busts of Roman emperors, a rocking-horse, two dolls' houses, a wooden horse and cart, African masks, birdcages and Victorian chamber pots and – exactly what they were looking for, a narrow mirror off a wardrobe.

'A lot of rubbish!' exclaimed Odd.

'That's just like grown-ups,' observed Elsewhere. 'Anything they no longer need they throw away. They don't stop to think that someone else might have a use for it.'

'How shall we get the mirror downstairs?' asked Odd.

'All we have to do,' explained Elsewhere, 'is tear up some rags and tie them around the mirror to make bumpers, then we'll slide it downstairs.'

Staircase by staircase, round and round, sweating and struggling they edged and eased the mirror until they had reached the staircase leading down to the main hall. They were just lowering it down the last flight of stairs when the gong rang loudly for the midday meal. Odd was so startled that he let go of the mirror, and in an instant it bumped its way down to the bottom of the stairs and smashed into smithereens. As the sound of the crash reverberated throughout the house, doors

opened and clowns peered over railings from the landings above. There were cries of, 'What is it? What's the matter? Is anyone hurt?'

Odd sat on the stairs, tears splashing from his eyes. It was all so important to Elsewhere and now he had ruined it.

Everyone helped to sweep up and clear away the mess, but Odd was so upset that he could not eat his food, even though Elsewhere kept trying to tell him

that it did not matter as really he would not have had
enough time to rehearse a new act.

That night the big circus tent was a blaze of lights and
everyone was in a state of great excitement. A band
was playing and hundreds of clowns were filling up the
seats usually occupied by the public. Then, with a fanfare
of trumpets, the King entered his special box; the lights
were lowered, and the Entertainment had commenced.

The Entertainment was exactly like an ordinary

circus except that all the acts were performed by clowns. Whizz, Tizz and Phizz did a conjuring act. For their first trick they produced a box and held it up so that the audience could see that it was really empty. It had a lid at the top and another at the bottom so that Whizz could pass his arm through it and show that there was no false bottom to it.

The box was then closed.

'Hey presto!' they cried in unison.

Then, opening the box, Phizz drew out from it yards and yards of bright coloured silk. Once again the box was held up and shown to be empty.

'Mother Hubbard's cupboard is bare!' they sang.

Again the box was closed.

'Hey presto!' they cried.

This time Tizz opened it and with a flourish brought out a bouquet of coloured flowers. Again they held up an empty box to the audience. Again they cried, 'Mother Hubbard's cupboard is bare!' and closed the box.

'Hey presto!' they cried and Whizz, opening it, lifted out a white rabbit!

Now, to a roll of drums, a large red box was carried on and placed over Tizz's head. Whizz took sixteen daggers and one by one plunged them into the box from all directions. He then took a metal pole and plunged this in at the top, right through where Tizz's skull must be inside the box. The front was then removed and everyone could see the box full of daggers and the pole down the centre, but of Tizz's head there was not a sign! The box was closed up again. Whizz drew out the pole and the daggers and then, removing the front of the box, showed the audience Tizz's head unharmed.

For their last trick Whizz, Tizz and Phizz ran on with

three perches which they placed on pedestals in the centre of the ring. Tied to each perch was a large inflated balloon. Each of them took a wand.

'Abracadabra-Barbara-Sevila!' they cried and then, with their wands tapped the balloons which burst and there, inside each, standing on its perch, was a white dove!

So act followed act with equal brilliance and the audience generously applauded each. For there is no audience in the world so critical, and yet so appreciative, as an audience of professional entertainers. Like those in the ring, every member of the audience was a master of his craft.

Standing in the wings, watching, Elsewhere whispered to Odd, 'I don't think I stand a chance. I'm too much out of practice.'

Odd looked at him anxiously. 'Once you're out there, you'll enjoy it, you know you will. You won't have time to be nervous,' he said, trying to encourage him.

Tumbling acts were followed by ventriloquist acts. There were acts with dogs, monkeys, horses and elephants. There were dangerous acts with lions and tigers. And then, there was Coco.

For his act fifty tall cheval mirrors were carried on and placed around the arena. The lights were lowered and the band played a French tune. Slowly, through the central mirror, the audience could see, on the other side, the figure of Coco, all in white like Pierrot. He sat perched on a high stool, his head on one side, his arms flopping, like a marionette when the strings are slack. He was wearing the costume of Debureau who was as famous a clown in France as Grimaldi was in England.

He walked forwards and the mirror opened like a

73

door. As he stepped through, it swung back on its hinges and immediately he was reflected in all fifty mirrors. As he circled the arena, turning cartwheels, so fifty other Cocos seemed to be travelling round the ring with him. Suddenly the audience burst out into tumultuous applause. At first Odd was slow to realise what was happening. Coco went on circling the ring, but, one by one, the reflections disappeared until there was only one mirror reflecting him. And then that reflection also vanished.

'I'm glad I didn't do my vanishing act,' whispered Elsewhere. 'I'm glad we had that accident.'

Coco continued performing handsprings and cartwheels and backflips, faster and faster. Then one mirror, then another, now here, now there, began to reflect him until, once again, all fifty mirrors were reflecting the image of Coco the Clown. Suddenly, and Odd gasped – he just could not see how it was done, Coco himself vanished, yet his reflections, all fifty of them, went on performing.

The audience rose to its feet, roaring applause. Even Elsewhere was shouting and hurrahing, he had forgotten his nerves and his jealousy.

'Oh, he's the best!' he cried. 'He's truly the best.'

As Coco re-appeared in the centre of the ring, all the reflections vanished and he stood alone, a solitary white figure, acknowledging the tremendous ovation of the excited audience.

More acts followed until, at long last, it was Elsewhere's turn. The circus hands rolled on two dozen large white rubber balls. Elsewhere jumped on to each, rotating them swiftly with his toes, so that they were set gliding about the ring like dodgems at the fair. Faster and faster and faster they spun with Elsewhere stepping from ball to ball until suddenly, he slipped and fell flat on his face. The audience gasped. Elsewhere rolled over and pretended it had been a deliberate mistake, but Odd could see that he was shaken.

Now long slim poles were brought on, and Odd himself carried on a pile of tin plates. Elsewhere proceeded to place a plate on the end of each pole, set it spinning, and then balanced each pole on one of the white balls. Soon the whole arena was a forest of gliding balls, waving wands, and spinning discs.

Elsewhere put a whistle to his mouth and blew sharply. The balls stopped moving, the tin plates balancing delicately on the ends of the poles. Elsewhere waved his wand and there was a roll of drums.

Everyone waited expectantly.

But nothing happened.

Odd held his breath and wished hard. The plates were supposed to fly through the air and pile up on Elsewhere's hand that held the wand. Inside the wand there was a magnet. Odd could see the beads of sweat on Elsewhere's white, strained face. Perhaps he should have used a stronger magnet.

Again Elsewhere waved his wand and there was a roll of drums.

Again the audience waited expectantly.

Then one of the plates toppled and fell with a clatter to the floor. Swiftly, one after the other, like ninepins, all the plates and poles tumbled to the ground.

There were tears in Odd's eyes. But Elsewhere was bravely bowing with a great flourish and pretending it was all part of the act.

There was a spattering of applause like scattered raindrops. Everyone felt very sorry for Elsewhere. The circus hands quickly cleared the ring and the next act was announced. Odd realised that Elsewhere had failed badly with his first chance. He turned to look for him, but there was no sign of him anywhere. He had vanished.

It was not so much that Elsewhere had run away; it was that he had just walked away into the night. Anything to get away. He could feel one of his dark moods coming on and he knew that he needed to be on his own. It hurt him to realise how much it now meant to him to win. More than that, there was also a deep sense of failure. The motto of the clowns was *One good turn deserves another*, but his first turn had not been good, so how could his second be any better?

He turned to look back at the blaze of lights in Tippity House and, beyond it, at the luminous shape of the Big Top. Perched on the pinnacle was a large red ball so that the roof of the tent looked like a clown's cap with a bobble on top. Above this towered high king poles with giant steel ropes taking the strain of the tent. He could hear the music playing, punctuated by bursts of applause. Suddenly he leaned forward. Stumbling up through the trees came a small round figure. It was Odd.

'Oh, there you are!' said Odd cheerfully. 'I thought you might be having one of your moods.'

'What do you mean?' replied Elsewhere sharply. At the very least he expected some sympathy.

'Well, you know,' laughed Odd, 'having messed it up and all, you're bound to feel disappointed.' Odd knew that the important thing was never to give in to Elsewhere's moods.

'It's more than that!' grunted Elsewhere. 'I'll never be King now. I've ruined my chances.'

''Course you haven't!' replied Odd brightly. 'I knew you would say that, but you've still got another chance, remember. So, if at first you don't succeed, try, try again!'

Elsewhere stared at him.

'That's funny,' he murmured, 'that's what Robert Bruce, King of Scotland said.'

'Did he?' replied Odd. 'I've never met him.'

'No, I mean that's where the expression originated,' and then he told Odd the story, just as Hamish had told it to him. After this he felt more cheerful.

'What are you going to do for your act tomorrow?' asked Odd.

'I don't know,' he replied.

'What about your acrobatics on the trapeze? You know that's your best trick.'

'But I'm so out of practice.'

'All right,' replied Odd promptly, 'then let's rig up ropes and trapezes in the trees first thing tomorrow morning and rehearse all day.'

Slowly, with Odd's help, Elsewhere was beginning to perk up and to think really hard about his second chance.

'Even though I'll never be King now at least I'll show them how good I can be.'

'That's right!' grinned Odd.

The next morning the orchard at the end of the kitchen garden was rigged up like a gymnasium. Ropes dangled from high branches or stretched from tree to tree, while Odd helped Elsewhere make trapezes out of lengths of rope and walking sticks. Soon Elsewhere was swinging through the trees like Tarzan, and Odd was applauding excitedly.

Suddenly Odd said, 'We ought to have something else, to make the act different from any other acrobatic act.'

Elsewhere, hanging from a rope by one hand, called down, 'You mean like if I were to play the violin as I swung upside down?'

'Yes,' laughed Odd.

'Only I can't play the violin!' answered Elsewhere.

'Perhaps you could breathe fire?' suggested Odd. 'It's quite easy. All you have to do is take a mouthful of paraffin, spit it out and hold a match to it as you spit.'

'But I'd be so high up I'd probably set fire to the roof!'

'Yes, there is that, I suppose,' replied Odd thoughtfully.

'I know!' said Elsewhere, swinging across to another tree.

'What?'

'You could release hundreds of white doves and they'd all fly up.'

'But how would we ever get them back afterwards?' asked Odd.

'And besides, they'd fly all over the audience and you know what would happen!'

'Well, the audience could have umbrellas! I tell you what though,' added Elsewhere slithering down a rope in his excitement,' you could blow lots and lots of soap bubbles and then they'd reflect the light like lots of mirrors –'

'Oh, I say!' gasped Odd.

'What?'

'I've just had a marvellous idea. What did you do with all that broken glass from yesterday?'

'It's in the dust-bins.'

'And where would I find those large white balls you used?'

'They are kept in the prop-room, backstage,' replied Elsewhere. 'Why?'

'Never you mind!' grinned Odd. 'You go back to your practising!'

And with that he hurried off importantly. He got out the tricycle and pedalled into the village to buy some glue, three dozen bars of soap, some razor blades, and fourteen clay pipes. Then he disappeared into one of the stables.

All that afternoon, behind locked doors and a notice that announced

BEAR AT WURK KEPE OUT!

he could be heard sawing and hammering and smashing glass.

That evening they were all gathered once again in the Big Top. Only this time the atmosphere was much more tense. Backstage, people's nerves were on edge and out front the audience was quieter, more hushed with expectancy.

Whizz, Tizz and Phizz did more conjuring tricks while Coco did a fast juggling act with what seemed to be hundreds of small white balls. He made upside down U shapes as well as figures of eight; they flashed by so fast that they looked like white bulbs flicking on and off.

'It's so professional,' murmured Elsewhere in admiration. 'It's so well rehearsed that you know he could never make a mistake.'

'I think perhaps it might be almost too good,' observed Odd quietly. 'Perhaps a mistake every now and then really makes it more exciting, because then the audience can see how difficult it is. With Coco you feel nothing ever could go wrong.'

When Coco took his bow there was tremendous applause. Odd stole a glance at Elsewhere when he did not know he was being observed. He could see that he was worried and thinking, if only I hadn't mucked it up the first time.

And now, once again, it was Elsewhere's turn. The circus hands were hurrying on with buckets of soapy water.

Elsewhere cartwheeled into the arena. As he saw Odd approaching, he called out, 'Hullohullohullohullo! Who are you then?'

ODD: *I'm Odd.*
ELSEWHERE: *Come again?*
ODD: *I'm Odd.*

Elsewhere turned to the audience and said,

ELSEWHERE: *He's odd all right!*
ODD: *No, no, I mean my name is Odd.*
ELSEWHERE: *Your name is odd? Why, what's wrong with it?*
ODD: *There's nothing wrong with it. It's just that it is – Odd.*

ELSEWHERE: *Is your needle stuck or something?*
ODD: *I mean my name is Odd.*

Odd then began to sing:

> *I'm O double D, I'm Odd.*
> *I know I am,*
> *I'm sure I am*
> *I'm O double D, I'm ODD.*

ELSEWHERE: *My friend here,*
He's just a bear.
Now ain't that odd!
ODD (singing): *I'm Odd.*
ELSEWHERE (singing): *He's Odd.*
ODD (speaking): *What's your name?*
ELSEWHERE: *I'm Elsewhere.*
ODD: *How can you be elsewhere when*
you're here?
ELSEWHERE (singing): *I'm – Elsewhere;*
Else, who do you think I am?
I ain't the King of Clapham,
Nor the Emp'ror of Siam;
But, wherever I am,
Wherever I am,
I'm sure to be – Elsewhere!
ODD (singing): *I'm Nobod*
But a Bear called Odd,
A Bear that's very Mod!
ELSEWHERE (singing): *I'm Elsewhere.*
I haven't a care,
There's nothing I fear!
ODD: *I'm a most unusual bear*
ELSEWHERE: *He's a most unusual bear*

ODD: *He's a clown that's top of the town!*

ELSEWHERE: *I'm a clown that's Top of the Town.*

BOTH TOGETHER: *It's Odd and Elsewhere, come to town!*

Now Odd and Elsewhere took two pipes that Odd had made especially from seven clay pipes attached to a central tube. He and Elsewhere each had one. They dipped them into the buckets of soapy water and began blowing bubbles. They each blew seven bubbles, which made fourteen bubbles at a time. Fourteen times two is twenty-eight, counted Odd:

$$14 \times 3 \text{ is } 42,$$
$$14 \times 4 \text{ is } 56,$$
$$14 \times 5 \text{ is } 70,$$
$$14 \times 6 \text{ is } 84,$$
$$14 \times 7 \text{ is } \ldots \text{ is } \ldots \text{ is.} \ldots$$

Odd gave up counting, he just went on blowing bubbles.

From the roof was lowered a globe which Odd had made from the hundreds of tiny fragments of broken mirror stuck on to one of the white balls. All the lights were turned off except for some coloured lights on the ball. Slowly it began to turn and, as it did so, thousands of beads of light spun round the tent, speckling and dazzling the audience. The bubbles, reflecting the many colours, floated upwards like butterflies.

Elsewhere climbed up a rope ladder until he was on a level with the high wire. He began to swing from trapeze to trapeze, somersaulting in mid-flight, looping the loop, until the air seemed filled with flying figures as of

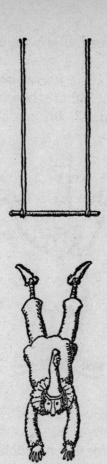

many clowns, crossing and inter-crossing, flecked with swirling lights and soap bubbles bursting their rainbow colours.

At the climax, the music stopped. Elsewhere, high up under the roof, swung idly by one hand.

'Is it supper-time?' he called out to Odd far below.

'Yes!' answered Odd.

'Right, coming down now!' replied Elsewhere and,

head first, he dropped like a stone, zooming down towards the ring.

The audience gasped in horror because there was no safety net. At the last minute, however, he gave a twist of his body, and landed lightly on his feet.

There was a sound like that of waves crashing on a pebbly seashore, as the whole audience rose to its feet, including the King, roaring its applause.

Elsewhere walked round the ring, acknowledging the cheers, finally coming to stand beneath the royal box. With a splendid flourish he removed his cap, bowing deeply to the King.

Odd bowed too, standing at a distance. And his heart swelled with pride. Even if Elsewhere had ruined his chances and never became King of the Clowns, he knew that his friend was a great performer on the trapeze. He was a star.

The Entertainment was over and one by one the King had sent for each clown. Elsewhere had been the very last to be called. It was already dusk. From the roof of the caravan hung a ship's lantern, its flame mirrored in the many horse brasses that lined the walls. The outside of the caravan was painted all over in bright colours with flowers and fishes, butterflies and birds.

'There'll be a nip in the air with the sun gone,' said the King. 'Put some more wood on the fire, will you?'

Elsewhere lifted the porcelain top of the old stove and put in some sticks. He then crossed to the half door of the caravan and leaned out. Around camp fires groups of clowns were singing, teaching each other new songs. Tippity House in the background was a blaze of lights, while overhead the first stars pricked out their patterns one by one. Near by, a small group was singing the old Welsh song, *Myfanwy*.

'I've had all sorts of exciting adventures,' said Elsewhere, talking almost to himself, while the King listened, sucking at his now empty pipe. 'I've been in many places, met many people. I've known what it is to be famous and what it is to be forgotten. Yet I could never feel that any of it was permanent. I could never really believe in any of it. I enjoyed it but always I had the feeling that it could not last. Not in any sad way, but just that things have a way of changing. Nothing ever stays the same. And so I got to feeling that wherever I was I could just as easily be elsewhere. That's how I got my name, of course. Odd has always felt the odd man out, too. I suppose that's why we understand each other so well.'

He turned to look back at the King. 'And then I've always had this feeling that somewhere, elsewhere, something was waiting for me, and that when I found it, then I wouldn't any more feel lost. I'd be *here* and not *elsewhere*.'

The King chuckled. His eyes glowed darkly in the shadows and the lamplight.

'And you were right. You are *here*. And something *is* waiting for you,' he said. He got up and moved across to Elsewhere. 'You see, I am going to name you as my successor!'

At first Elsewhere was so astonished that he could not speak. Outside there was the sound of the singing and the laughter, while here, inside the King's caravan, all was quiet and still.

'But I was so clumsy!' he replied. 'And I made all those mistakes. Surely it ought to be Coco. He's a great clown. He's the best!'

'It isn't altogether being the best performer that counts,' answered the King. 'Although there's no one to match you on the trapeze! But what also counts is the way you coped with your mistakes, the way in which you improvised. Others might have given up in despair,

or sulked. But you carried on that first evening as though nothing had gone wrong. You made it look almost as though the mistakes had been on purpose, to make us laugh. And that's important if one is to be King. Things often go wrong and when that happens you have to know how to carry on and not despair.'

Elsewhere nodded. 'If at first you don't succeed,' he said, 'try, try again!'

'That's it!' answered the King, smiling.

Elsewhere sat silent and overawed. He wondered whether being King would mean becoming solemn and serious and perhaps rather dull?

The King chuckled. 'I know what is going through your mind,' he said, 'because I had exactly the same thoughts when I learned that I was to be King. I thought it meant putting on a straight face, having to act a part all the time, and never being able to be my real self. But it isn't like that at all. There are responsibilities, of course. But one is King of the *Clowns*, remember. It wouldn't do for the King to lose his sense of humour, would it?'

With that, the King took off his wig and rubbed some cream over his face, removing his make-up. As Elsewhere watched, it was as though the King's mask were melting and he saw, through the make-up, the worn and wrinkled skin of an old man, the shadows under the tired but kindly eyes. He realised that he was seeing the King as no one else had ever seen him, at the end of the day, tired and alone.

'It is a lonely task being King,' he continued. 'I wouldn't have you think it was all fun. They all think it's just a lot of parades and processions and being top of the bill. I dare say you thought the same, too?'

Elsewhere blushed, and then grinned.

'But as King you are father of a big unruly family. It's like trying to control a litter of puppies. They all want to go in different directions!'

'Why do you have to retire?' asked Elsewhere. 'Why can't you go on being King?'

'It's time for me to retire. It will be the same for you one day, you will just know the time has come. Besides, there's a new generation of clowns coming up, and they need a leader who is perhaps closer to them than I am.'

'What will you do when you retire?'

'I don't know yet. The moment one ceases to be King one no longer has power. As a leader you have power, but that power has nothing to do with you as a person. It goes with the job of being King.'

He paused. 'You'll make a good King,' he continued, 'because you won't be deceived into believing the power to be your own. The power belongs to the office and not to the person. The power that the King wields is to be exercised for others and never for himself.'

Elsewhere nodded. 'When one moment you've been top of the bill,' he answered, 'and the next, thrown away in a cupboard and forgotten, as I was, you learn not to take yourself too seriously!'

The King laughed. 'It's like the motto in your cracker, *Aim high, there is plenty of room to fall!* You're right. It doesn't do to get too carried away with your own importance just because you are top of the bill or top of the class.'

'It's like my song,' added Elsewhere. 'One day you are up, and one day you are down, that's what it is to be a clown! Would you like to hear my song?'

The King smiled. 'Yes, very much. Everyone has his own special song. When the time comes for you to take over from me, I shall teach you my song. That is the Secret of Tippity-Witchit, the secret that one King passes on to another. And now, let's hear your song!'

After he had sung his song, Elsewhere sat quietly.

'What are you thinking now?' asked the King.

'I was thinking about Odd. You see, he will want to know how I got on, and if I'm supposed not to tell him, if it is meant to be a secret, I'm afraid lest he should read my thoughts. Sometimes he knows me better than I do myself!'

The King smiled. 'A secret can be shared by more than one or two people. Did you not know that? Besides, a friend is someone with whom one can share a secret. I have a feeling that Odd is going to stand you in good stead over the years. You are lucky to have him for a friend. You see, you are very excitable, full of enthusiasm and ideas. But you have to learn not to get carried away quite so much! Odd has got his feet firmly on the ground. He is very steady and reliable. Try and listen to him a little more often, eh?'

Elsewhere looked up. It was funny how the King seemed always to know so much. It was as though he, too, could read your thoughts.

The King got up and went to a cupboard. He took out a bottle of wine and poured out two glasses.

'Why don't you and Odd start up a little circus of your own?' he said suddenly. 'Travel it around. Try and learn as many new things as you can. Every kind of experience is valuable, especially for a King, because he has to know so much about other people. Then, when

the time comes, you will be ready to take on an even bigger Circus. Let us drink to that, shall we? – as one King to a future King!'

Then, after a pause, he added, 'Oh, by the way, I have been invited to have tea with you and Odd tomorrow at the Granary. Arbuthnot is going to collect us after lunch. And he says to tell you that your other friends have arrived, Collander Moll and Hallelujah. And now I think you had better go and break the news to Odd. But remember, he is the *only* one to know and you must stress it upon him how important a secret it is!'

That next afternoon at the Granary, Collander Moll acted as 'mother', serving tea for everyone except Odd who had milk. In the centre of the table stood an enormous cake, the kind that is crowded with fruit and nuts, moist with brandy and rum, heavy with almond paste, and crusted all over with chunky white icing, inset with whole crystallised fruits.

'It's called Umfreville Cake,' announced Mr Goodman, 'and it's made from an old recipe that Arbuthnot found in the attics. We advertise it as "the cake to last a year" – present company excepted,' he added with a wink.

After tea, Odd and Elsewhere took Collander Moll, Hallelujah Jones, the King of the Clowns, and Collander Moll's auntie, Miss Myfanwy, on a tour of the Granary. They showed them Mr Goodman's famous collection of butterflies, and they stopped in the stables to talk to Tipsy and give her some lumps of sugar.

When they got back to the house it was time to return to Llandrindod Wells.

'Oh, can't we stay a little longer?' pleaded Odd.

94

'No,' answered Collander Moll. 'We've got to think about getting back to London. And you two are coming with us on the train. You're not going back in that caravan. Mr Goodman has very kindly offered to give Tipsy a home here.'

'But couldn't you and Hallelujah come in the caravan with us?' suggested Elsewhere suddenly.

Collander Moll cocked her head on one side like a bird.

'You see,' said Elsewhere, pressing his point, 'we've got this idea for a circus which would help to raise money for the National Trust!'

Odd could see that Collander Moll was impressed by this.

'Well, now,' she replied, not knowing what to say. Then she turned to Hallelujah. 'Why not, Dad?' – not that Hallelujah had spoken a word. 'After all, you don't like that old train, with all those stops and changes between here and London. And we don't really need to be back for another week, now I think about it. You'd enjoy being at the reins. It'd be like the old days when you used to do your postman's round in the pony and trap. It'd be a bit of a holiday to be out in the open air.'

They could all see that she was very taken with the idea.

Then she turned and looked sharply at Elsewhere. 'What do you mean – *circus*? We're not taking a lot of dirty animals with us!'

So then Elsewhere explained his plan. He and Odd would do an act, sing some songs, and perform some conjuring tricks.

'And when we came to a town, Hallelujah could go ahead ringing a bell and shouting, O-yez! O-yez! like a town crier!'

'And I could have a drum to beat!' laughed Odd. 'And Elsewhere could have a trumpet to blow!'

'Oh, yes, he'd do that very well,' grunted Hallelujah. 'Sort of comes natural to him to blow his own trumpet!'

'And whistles to blow!' added Elsewhere.

'And rattles to rattle,' said Odd.

'And Collander Moll could dress up in old curtains and pretend to be a gipsy,' suggested Elsewhere, 'and tell fortunes.'

'Oh, could I?' replied Collander Moll.

'And I could do a juggling act with treacle tarts!' said Odd, jumping up and down.

'And who's going to clean up the mess after you, lad?' grumbled Hallelujah.

'And Collander Moll could bake Odd and Elsewhere gingerbread men,' said Elsewhere, 'like she did when I was ill in hospital once. And we could sell them. And Odd could make some of his fudge.'

'And we could do a shadow play behind a sheet,' suggested Odd.

'And a puppet show,' added Elsewhere.

'And you could have a magic lantern with some slides of Goldilocks and the Three Bears,' suggested Mr Goodman, joining in the fun.

'And there's that old gramophone with the horn in the attics,' said Arbuthnot. 'They could play a record of *The March of the Gladiators* as they came into town.'

'And we could paint across the caravan,' said Elsewhere, 'the words – *Odd and Elsewhere Come To Town!*'

'And we could fly kites with our names on them,' laughed Odd.

'And-and-and-and-and!' said Collander Moll all of a sudden. 'If we are to get any of this done before next Christmas we'd better get ourselves organised. Now, Elsewhere, if you are going to be in charge of this, you'd better make a list, and tell us what we are each supposed to do. And then you and Odd will have to rehearse your act.'

So they had a planning conference. Several of the young people offered to paint the outside of the caravan. Arbuthnot brought down from the attics the magic lantern and the gramophone, as well as a toy trumpet and some whistles. Collander Moll and her auntie spent the next day baking gingerbread men, while Hallelujah brushed and groomed Tipsy and plaited her mane with brightly coloured ribbons. Miss Myfanwy also found some ostrich feathers and made these into a head-dress for Tipsy.

The next day they were all busy putting the last

finishing touches to the caravan when the Granary bell
went clang-clang-clang!

'Goodness, who can that be?' said Mr Goodman. 'It
sounds very important, whoever it is.'

They all turned and trooped down the drive to the
front door of the Granary. There, tugging away at the
bell on its long wire, was a small clown, aged about
eight, holding a very important looking envelope.
Leaning against the house was a tricycle.

'Very important message, sir,' he piped. 'For Mr
Odd, sir. Yes, sir!' He put the envelope in his mouth
and turned a somersault.

'Who is it from?' asked Odd.

The small clown removed the letter from his mouth and stood the right way up.

'From the King, sir. That's who. Are you Mr Odd, sir?'

Everyone stood round watching while Odd took the letter. He held the envelope between his paws.

'Oh, do hurry up and open it!' said Elsewhere.

'It's my paws,' replied Odd. 'They aren't very good for opening letters.'

So Arbuthnot opened it for him. And then Odd read –

Dear Odd,
In recognition of your services in the Ring,
I have pleasure in making you an Honorary Clown
for life.

Your Friend, The King of the Clowns.

'What does Honorary mean?' asked Odd, gazing at the letter in awe.

'It means you don't have to pay anything,' replied Mr Goodman.

'I say!' said Odd. 'I say!'

Then he turned to Elsewhere with a grin and gave him a push. 'Now I'm a clown, too,' he said, 'I can boss you around!'

'No, you can't,' answered Elsewhere, 'because . . .' and then he stopped. He put his hand to his mouth and stared in horror at Odd. He had nearly let out his secret.

'Because?' said Collander Moll. 'Because what?'

'Because I'm bigger than he is!' laughed Elsewhere.

And so at last they got on board the caravan. And with a ringing of bells and a blowing of trumpets they set off on their return journey to London.

THE END

Fenton House in Hampstead, London, belongs to the National Trust, and is open to the public. The National Trust, which was founded in 1894, helps to save and preserve the nation's historic houses, castles, gardens and thousands of acres of land that might otherwise be lost or destroyed.

You can see more Magnet Books on the following pages:

James Roose-Evans

THE ADVENTURES OF ODD AND ELSEWHERE

One morning a small bear called Odd wakes up to
see the removal van drive away. 'The odds are,'
he murmurs to himself, 'that I am the only person
left in this house, and what could be odder than
that?' But he soon has very odd company indeed
when he finds a circus clown called Elsewhere hanging
upside-down in a cupboard. The two friends decide to
team up and go and live in Fenton House, next door.
This is just the start of Odd and Elsewhere's
extraordinary adventures together.

THE SECRET OF THE SEVEN BRIGHT SHINERS

Odd and Elsewhere visit their friends in charge
of the British Rail Lost Property Office. But it has
been burgled! The two friends set off on the trail of the
thieves and discover an important clue, the gang's
secret password – The Seven Bright Shiners.

ODD AND THE GREAT BEAR

Odd is very worried as he does not know what kind of
bear he is, who he is, or where he came from.
So he bravely sets out alone on a daring adventure
to find the legendary Great Bear who lies sleeping in
Bear Mountain and guards the secret of the Lost
Treasure of Wales. Surely the Great Bear will be
able to tell Odd who he really is?

Pictures by Brian Robb

Mary Welfare

WITCHDUST

Who are the two scatty old ladies, often seen
jogging in moleskin tracksuits, and why do strange
things start to happen in the village? Gladys and
Victoria are just two harmless witches – or are they?
What has become of their magic powers? Only
their cat, Miss Wiggs, knows the answer – the
secret of *Witchdust*.

Illustrated by Shirley Hughes

0 416 21390 1

Donald Bisset

WHAT TIME IS IT, WHEN IT ISN'T?

What is time? Where does it go? Why is it
different times at different places at the same time?
A group of unusual characters get very tied up
in knots trying to sort it all out, but have great fun
untangling themselves and helping the reader to
explore this difficult concept.

0 416 20830 4

JOHNNY THE TIN TORTOISE

Johnny sets off to visit a papier-mâché dragon, but he
can't go in a straight line. A pelican takes him
to Waterloo where he catches a train to the ninth
century. He meets King Alfred, a Dark Horse and
many others before he finally reaches the dragon!

0 416 24440 8

Ruth Manning-Sanders

A BOOK OF WITCHES

Witches don't fly on broomsticks – some ride stalks of
ragwort, or even old jars. They can conjure up
tempests and turn themselves and other people into
pigs, geese, or anything they please. Some are very
beautiful, but most of them are ugly, hump-backed
hags with hooked noses and evil, cackling
laughs, and all are up to no good . . .

A BOOK OF GHOST AND GOBLINS

Goblins are unpleasant little creatures who play wicked
tricks on people by night and day. But they
aren't as hair-raising as the disembodied spirits . . . the
ghosts who walk the earth at night and scare the
living daylights out of people.

A BOOK OF MONSTERS

Monsters are huge, hideous and ugly; they are hated and feared and people run screaming at the sight of them. Most of them are bad and brutal: their one wish is to eat as much as they can – especially tasty humans . . .

A BOOK OF WIZARDS

Wizards have amazing magic powers – they can change themselves into animals, birds, beggars or gipsies. And though some have good intentions, others are evil – like the wicked wizard in *Aladdin*. Usually they can outwit everyone, but occasionally even a wizard can make a silly mistake . . .

All illustrated by Robin Jacques

GILLIAN BAXTER

Pantomime Ponies

When Angela and Ian came to stay with their
unknown uncle in London, they find two pantomime
ponies, Magic and Moonshine, in the back yard.

Save the Ponies!

Angela and Ian are very upset when Uncle Arthur
has to find new stabling for the ponies. But eventually
the ponies themselves provide the answer.

Ponies by the Sea

Angela and Ian are pleased when the pantomime ponies
are booked for six weeks in a seaside summer show. But
Angela starts to feel out of things when Ian makes
friends with some other theatrical children.

Ponies in Harness

When a friend of Uncle Arthur's suggests Magic and
Moonshine enter a driving competition, everyone is
terribly excited, especially Angela.

Special Delivery

Two girls and a boy spend their spare time helping a
young man who runs a delivery round. When he has
an accident, the children try to carry on, helped by a
temperamental donkey.

Illustrated by Elizabeth Grant

HUMOUR

Nonsense verse selected by WILLIAM COLE

Oh What Nonsense!
Oh That's Ridiculous!
Beastly Boys and Ghastly Girls
Oh How Silly!

Each book has a selection of funny absurd and truly ridiculous rhymes accompanied by hilarious drawings – guaranteed to make you giggle!

Illustrated by Tomi Ungerer

ANN THWAITE (Ed.)

All Sorts of Poems

A collection of lively and amusing verse about all sorts of things – people, animals, birds, nonsense – including poems by James Fenton and Russell Hoban.

Illustrated by Patricia Mullins

Kenneth Grahame

THE WIND IN THE WILLOWS

Illustrated by Ernest H. Shepard

The story of Mole, Rat, Badger and Toad vividly
brought to life by E. H. Shepard's beautiful,
classic black and white line illustrations.

A. A. Milne

TOAD OF TOAD HALL

The famous stage adaptation of *The Wind in The
Willows*. Children who have delighted in the joys
and lovable characters of the classic story can act out
the adventures for themselves in this play.

These and other Magnet Books are available at your bookshop or newsagent. In case of difficulties, orders may be sent to:

Magnet Books
Cash Sales Department
PO Box 11
Falmouth
Cornwall TR10 9EN
England

Please send cheque or postal order, no currency, for purchase price quoted and allow the following for postage and packing:

U.K. CUSTOMERS
40p for first book, plus 18p for the second book and 13p for each additional book ordered, to a maximum charge of £1.49p.

B.F.P.O. and EIRE
40p for the first book, plus 18p for the second book and 13p per copy for the next 7 books, thereafter 7p per book.

OVERSEAS CUSTOMERS
60p for the first book, plus 18p per copy for each additional book.

While every effort is made to keep prices low, it is sometimes necessary to increase prices at short notice. Magnet Books reserve the right to show new retail prices on covers which may differ from those previously advertised in the text or elsewhere.